HECTOR'S SHELL

Dedicated to the memory of
Stephen Graham and Alex Mitchell

little bee books
An imprint of Bonnier Publishing Group
853 Broadway, New York, New York 10003
Copyright © 2015 by Thomas Radcliffe
First published by The Five Mile Press 2015. This little bee books edition 2015.
LITTLE BEE BOOKS is a trademark of Bonnier Publishing Group, and associated
colophon is a trademark of Bonnier Publishing Group.
Manufactured in China 1214 LEO
First Edition 2 4 6 8 10 9 7 5 3 1
Library of Congress Control Number: 2014957616
ISBN 978-1-4998-0095-1

www.littlebeebooks.com
www.bonnierpublishing.com

HECTOR'S SHELL

By Thomas Radcliffe

little bee books

After a successful day of adventuring and exploring beneath the sea . . .

Hector the turtle discovered that things were not quite as he had left them.

HIS PRECIOUS SHELL WAS

MISSING!

Returning home without it would mean **BIG** trouble.

Hector could imagine exactly what his mom and dad would say:

"Where did you have it last?"

"Have you looked under your bed?"

"**WHY** can't you take better care of your things!"

So Hector set off to investigate.

He described his shell to nearby beachgoers and asked
if they had seen any suspicious shell-related activity.

BUT nobody had seen his shell.

A sympathetic whale suggested asking a lifeguard.

Hector thought informing the authorities sounded like a good idea.

But the lifeguard was very busy and just pointed to the lost and found.

Hector rummaged hopefully.

BUT there was

NO SIGN of his shell.

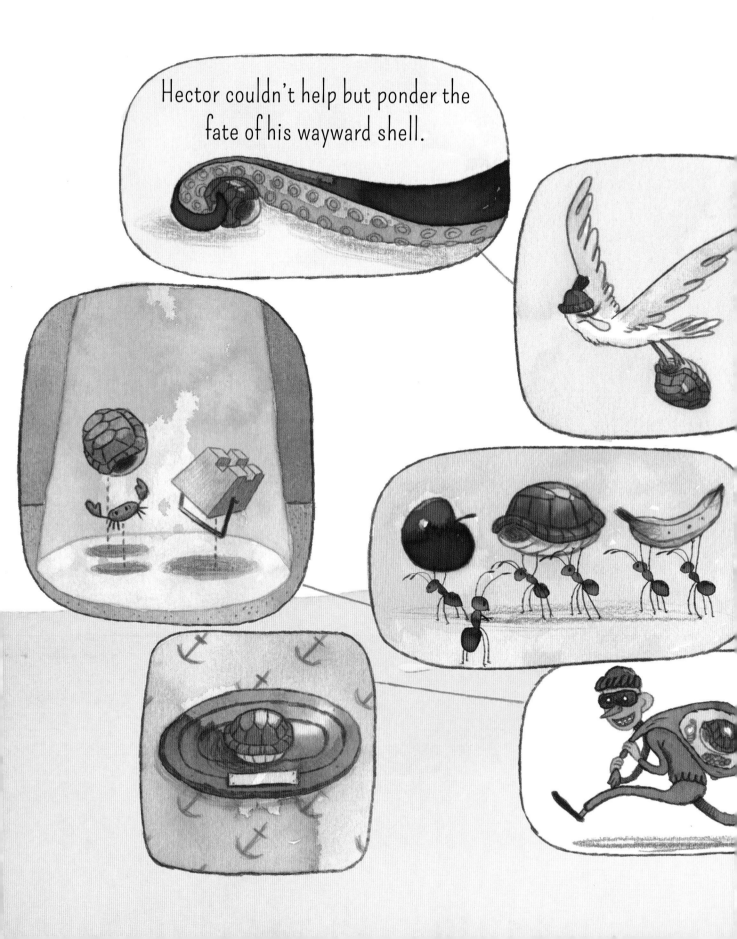

Hector couldn't help but ponder the fate of his wayward shell.

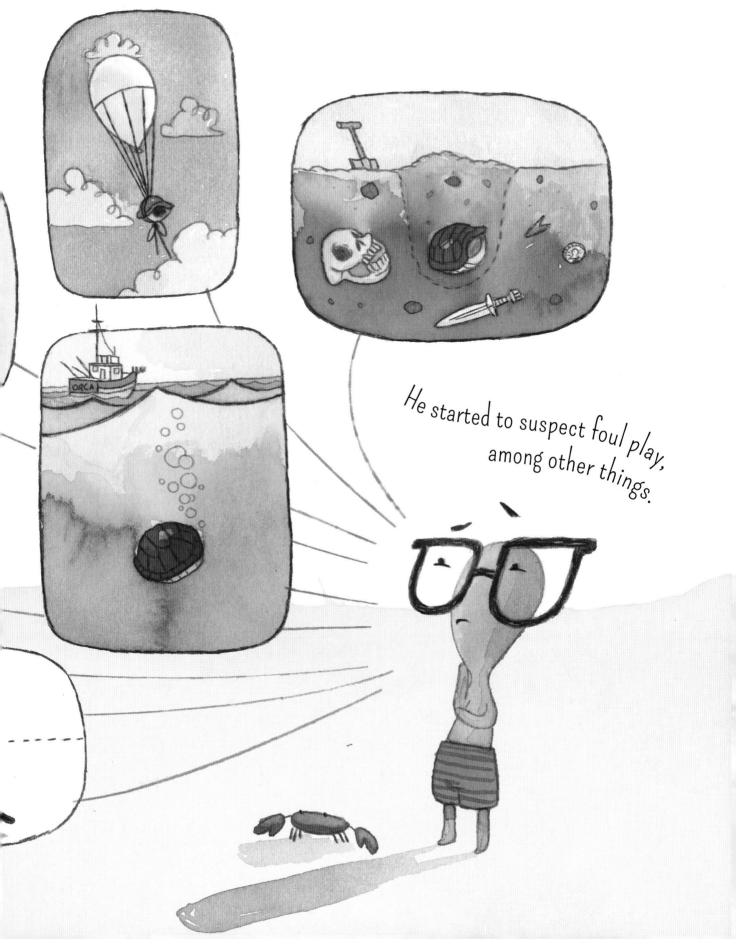

He started to suspect foul play, among other things.

Hector started to think that he might never find his shell.

"Maybe it is lost forever," Hector thought sadly.

But just then, a

REALLY GREAT IDEA

popped into Hector's head.

He would make himself a brand new shell,
even **BETTER** than his old one!

So Hector grabbed his bag
and went about collecting
things for shell-making....

He found old stuff...

odd stuff...

unwanted stuff...

and fun stuff.

Soon his bag was big and fat, and Hector decided it was time to start constructing.

First Hector tried transforming a shiny red beach bucket.

BUT the results were rather uncomfortable, and generally quite disappointing.

Then he tried folding some old newspaper into an origami shell.

BUT the newspaper was a bit soggy and covered Hector in mucky black ink.

A passerby kindly donated some balloons.

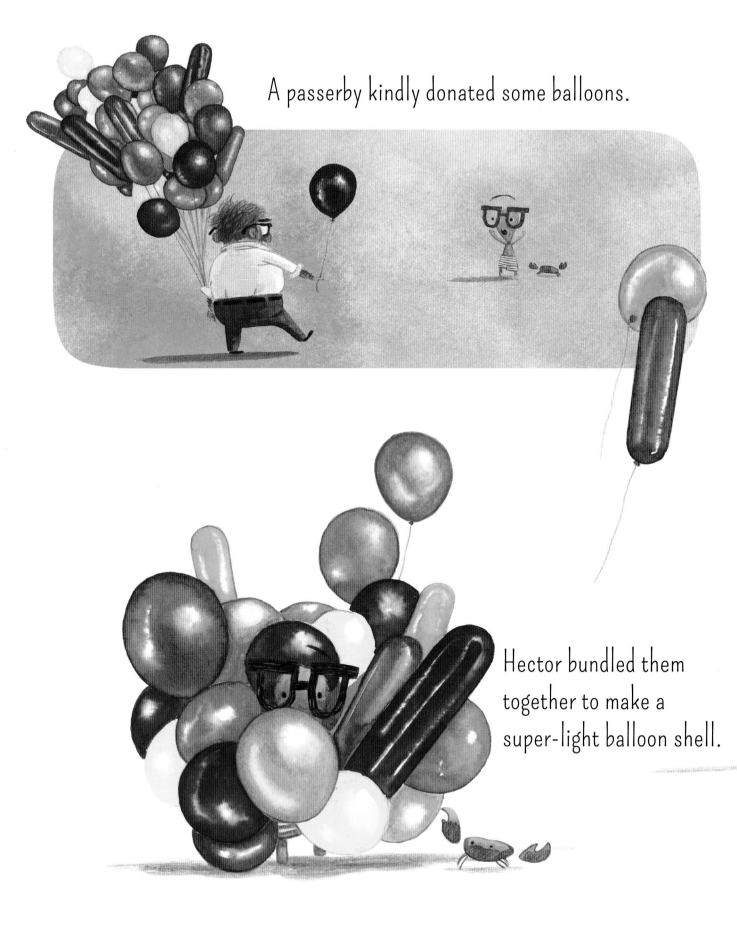

Hector bundled them together to make a super-light balloon shell.

BUT balloons,

it seemed,

did not make good shells.

POP

POP

POP

Hector lost all his balloons.

And then he lost his temper.

Hector stomped off in a **HUFF** and almost walked right past a handsome-looking seashell.

He thought it would make a splendid replacement shell!

BUT grumpy Mr. Hermit Crab was not feeling very generous.

He charged out of his shell, ranting and raving about private property and to **GET LOST PRONTO.**

Hector hurried away.

Hector decided he needed a bit of a rest.

Then he remembered the bag of stuff he had collected at the beginning of the shell fiasco. It was overflowing with all sorts of things he could try.

Hector tried slimy things . . .

and smelly things . . .

and smelly **AND** slimy things.

He tried shiny things . . .

shiny, noisy things . . .

BRrRRRt

and shiny, noisy, feathery things.

But nothing seemed quite right.
Then Hector stumbled upon something
buried in the sand dunes.

Hector couldn't believe his luck!

He tried on his fancy new shell, and noticed a BIG red button.

Which of course, he pressed right away.

Hector decided that shiny metal shells probably weren't right for him after all.

And just when he was about to give up and be a shell-less turtle forever, something caught his eye . . .

IT WAS HIS SHELL!

Right where he had left it for safekeeping,
in the sandcastle he had built!

"There's a lesson to be learned here," thought Hector.
But then the thought was gone.
"Maybe I'll have a yard sale tomorrow."

THE END